"This is my kind of book—fun, provocative and easy to read. Bob Leonard blends prose and poetry with a ring of authenticity true to the ear of a community journalist to give us a portrait of small-town life in Rural America, and its abiding wonders."
—Art Cullen, editor of *The Storm Lake Times*, Pulitzer Prize winner and author of the book, *Storm Lake: A Chronicle of Change, Resilience, and Hope from a Heartland Newspaper*

"An unexpectedly delightful collection of poems, reminiscences and whimsical reflections from native Iowan Robert Leonard. If that leads you to expect homespun tales with homely moralisms, be prepared to be surprised. Leonard's last lines almost always takes an unexpected turn, and what he gleans from his lifelong experiences is both modern and timeless. Though this could be a quick read, you'll find yourself stopping to meditate on many an unexpected twist in Leonard's storytelling and interpretations. Imagine that Millennials had a device in place of their phones, which instead of allowing them to capture an image or video of every instant of their lives, could capture how they felt and what they learned in the key moments of their lives. While that would be a technological marvel, it is exactly the skill that this eminently sharp observer of human foibles is able to deliver through his writing. If you're able to stop reading this compelling set of introspective jewels before you reach the end, you're far more disciplined than I can conceive!"
—Ricardo J. Salvador, Director and Senior Scientist, Food & Environment Program, Union of Concerned Scientists

"You don't have to have a PhD in anthropology to understand rural Iowa, but it helps. Reading *Deep Midwest* helps, too, and there is a lot for readers to understand. From the small-town bar owner who stops fights dead in their tracks by firing up his chainsaw, to the presidential candidate who has no idea what the locals mean by the low price of corn and beans,' to the luckless widow and mother of four small children whose husband commits suicide, these poems and stories about the Iowa countryside will tug at the reader's heart, sometimes plucking at its strings, sometimes tearing it in two, but most often causing it to soar—through stories about courage and even humor. And then there is love, the love of a father for his wife and children, or the love of an elderly couple—she with cancer and he with a heart condition—encouraging each other along on their daily walk inside Des Moines' Merle Hay indoor shopping mall. Dr. Robert Leonard has been many things in his life: an Iowa radio personality, a cab driver, a playwright, a university professor, a carpenter, a roofer, a champion heavyweight wrestler, and a journalist whose work has been in the *New York Times, Des Moines Register,* and *Kansas City Star.* 'Dr. Bob,' as he is called in Marion County, Iowa, has interviewed over 8,000 people along the way, and has a deep understanding of life in the rural Midwest, deepened even more by his doctorate in anthropology. His perspective on people, places, and events is not only influenced by education and experience but also tempered by love: love for a place and love for its people regardless of generation, political stance, or social status. As Dr. Leonard advises us all, 'Look for love, and when you find it, hold its warm and tender hand in your own, gently.'"
—James Blasingame, Professor, Department of English, Arizona State University

"Robert Leonard is a pseudonym for a guy I know named Dr. Bob. Dr. Bob is a suspendered radio reporter of a certain age who is curious to a fault. He hears and sees stuff the rest of us miss. And thank goodness he's taken the time to write some of it down. Loved the book."
—Harry Smith, NBC News

"With wit and a straight-forward passion, Robert Leonard writes of the tough and tender daily lives of the Midwestern working class. He captures the voices and vicissitudes of the barbers and bartenders, farmers and butchers, factory and maintenance workers who are trying to survive and find their balance within their families and communities in today's rural landscape. A poetry of the people, *Deep Midwest* rips off the fancy wrapping paper and gives you a glimpse of reality you may know, but never see captured elsewhere in literature."
—Mary Swander, former Iowa poet laureate, author, *Farmscape*

"Robert Leonard portrays life in Iowa vividly, with warmth and candor. Whether he describes rain filling the creek, a possum walking downhill, or creatively likens people to trees, I see it. As he expresses his appreciation for his wife, children, and the "road graders" out during blizzards, I feel it. As he ponders the thoughts of people who have crossed an old covered bridge, the thoughts of a red ant and the names of old farm equipment, I wonder, too. *Deep Midwest* is a wonderful way to see, feel, and think about Iowa and the Midwest."
—Rachelle Chase, author, *Lost Buxton*

"I loved reading Robert Leonard's *Deep Midwest: Midwestern Explorations*. His observations about everyday moments feel authentic and relatable—no matter where you live. His attention to detail so clearly stems from his work as an anthropologist and a reporter. I felt like I was right there with Bob: laying on the ice to check the depth of a frozen lake, bellied up to a dive bar in a small town, or even maneuvering my way through a political rally trying to grab a few moments with the next presidential hopeful. It is a book I intend to share with many."
—Lisa Carponelli, MSJ, associate professor at Simpson College

"Bob Leonard's *Deep Midwest* was not what I expected. I've known him for many years as one of Iowa's best journalists. His reporting has appeared in the *New York Times* and other national publications. He's been interviewed on national news programs, and his education and experience are always on display. He is an Iowa gem. Based on that journalism, I knew I would enjoy the "writing" in *Deep Midwest*. But this book is not journalism. It is a collection of some of the most brilliant and insightful poetry and creative prose I have read in years. My first reaction was that Bob was channeling William Carlos Williams. In some poems, deceptive simplicity led to profound insight. In others, the precise facts of everyday life were merely the prelude to a comic or tragic conclusion. I soon knew that *Deep Midwest* is the work of a man who loves his family, his town, and life in Iowa. His revelations are both personal and universal at the same time. How did I know I was in the presence of a gifted writer? Sitting next to my wife in bed, after I read a stunning line or passage, I would turn to her and say, 'You need to read this.' I was eager to watch her face as she experienced what I just felt, always pleased when her response was a whispered, 'Wow!'"
—Larry Baker, author, *A Good Man* and *The Flamingo Rising*

"Bob Leonard brings a father's heart and an anthropologist's eye to rural Iowa in *Deep Midwest*. Bob's sketches of small-town bars, solitary rambles, and family life in the country carry echoes of Ted Kooser and Linda Hasselstrom. His social commentary recalls Jack London's working-class themes. By turns intimate, lyrical, and satiric, *Deep Midwest* is difficult to classify but easy to love and sure to reshape a reader's assumptions about the Midwest."
—Joshua Doležal, author, *Down from the Mountaintop: From Belief to Belonging*

"From the momentary to the momentous, Robert Leonard holds a mirror up to the Midwest and casts a true reflection for all to see–from the Romantic to the real and the prosaic to the provocative. Here national politics occupies the mind, but so does re-roofing the shed. The farmer, the single mom, the meth addict, the dead soldier, the political pundit, and the bar stool philosopher are all here—shoulder to shoulder—sharing the open spaces of the prairie and sharing their stories."
—Dometa Brothers, author, *Cold Songs*

Deep Midwest

Robert Leonard

Ice Cube Press, LLC
North Liberty, Iowa, USA

Deep Midwest: Midwestern Explorations

Copyright © 2019 Robert Leonard

First Edition

Isbn 9781948509084

Library of Congress Control Number: On file with publisher

Ice Cube Press, LLC (Est. 1991)
North Liberty, Iowa 52317
www.icecubepress.com | steve@icecubepress.com

The paper used in this publication meets the minimum requirements of the American National Standard for Information Sciences—Permanence of Paper for Printed Library Materials, ANSI Z39.48-1992.

Project Intern and interior artwork: Kaylee Kirpes

Manufactured in USA

To Annie. Thanks for your wondrous gifts.

Table of Contents

Preface 1

Watermelon 12

Secretarial Migrations 15

Boy on Red Tractor 17

An Existential Question 19

122 Tornadoes 20

Mallet 22

Old Man in New Shoes 24

Target 25

Hometown Meats 27

Unlocked 28

Miller Lite 29

Bone Thin 30

Owl Tap 2007 32

Iowa Breadbasket 33

Hurricane 34

Bowl 36

Wired 37

Tonight's the Night 38

Small Miracles 40

Crazy Lady 43

Footprints 44

Cutting Wood 46

The Outdoor Channel 47

Not Yet 49

Joy 50

Robins I 53

Best Girl in the World 54

Deer Blind 55

Easter 58

Sheep Down 59

December 15, 2012 60

Maintainers 62

Playground 65

Buttered Bagel 66

Red Ant 68

Mona Lisa 72

Old Bridge 73

Promise 76

A Trip to Boston 78

Burying Annie's Dog 81

Winter's End 82

Insurance 83

Book Delivery 87

Lightnin' Bugs 89

Pulse 90

Workman's Comp 94

Robins II 95

Biscuits 97

Possum 98

Gifts 99

Air Conditioning 102

Archaeopteryx 104

Sunday Morning 105

Bar Fight 106

Girl Shoveling Snow 108
Ford's South End Tap 109
The Long Snake 111
A Great Many Iowans 114
Trust the Iowa Locals 117
Acknowledgments. 122
About the Author 125

PREFACE

My wife Annie, and our son and daughter, Asa and Johanna, moved from New Mexico where I taught anthropology at the University of New Mexico to southern Iowa in 2005. I grew up just north of Des Moines, and we decided it was time to get closer to my family, and raise our kids in rural Iowa. Asa was four years old, and Johanna was a baby when we arrived. We love New Mexico, and have kept in touch with family there the best we could, when you are half a continent away and have to work for a living. We love them, and miss them very much.

These stories and poems are, to me, simply moments of wonder I tried to capture. Such moments are all around us, every day. We just have to first notice, and then capture them. Paradoxically, both the hardest and the easiest part is to *decide* to capture the moment, and then take a note. Sometimes my notes are on scraps of paper, napkins, or the back of my hand. The note becomes a kind of temporal bookmark for my mind, a placeholder in life around which a memory or web of memories can later be constructed into a story or poem. Without a note, unless the moment is particularly noteworthy, it will go *poof.* As I like to say, my brain is leaky.

As I write these words, it's Thursday, February 7, 2019. I'm sitting at Smokey Row Coffee shop in Des Moines, it's ten degrees above zero, and as I look out of the window the row of world flags flying to the north of the coffee shop are being blasted by relentless twenty-five mph winds from the west. While the flags of Scandinavia seem to be doing fine, in my imagination the Brazilian flag is shivering. It's the kind of cold where you can feel the life being sucked out of you as you walk from the front door to the car, yet, maybe fifty people around me ventured outside to travel to the warmth of coffee, food, and companionship. Most seem to be college students, studying or working on projects together. Some people are conversing, but most are looking into their phone or computer, tapping away. I presume one meeting in the corner is about business, and a group of ladies well above retirement age have quietly settled into one another in a booth like warm, sleepy puppies.

At a table halfway across the coffee shop, a young political reporter I know who works for the Des Moines Register stares out the window into the cold for awhile, and then starts pecking at her keyboard, only to look outside again, thinking, before returning to her computer. I was curious what she was working on, but rather than bother her to satisfy my curiosity, I left her with a gift all writers crave, solitude when they are being productive.

To my right, a young woman with an angelic smile nurses her chubby, perfect blond baby, as she types on her iPhone. I am wondering what she is seeing or reading on her phone that is making her smile, when a rush of arctic air from my left blindsides me. A worker has opened the drive up window to take an order and a woman seated at an adjacent table and I share a nervous laugh, as the cold air hits us with a subzero blast.

A young perfectly groomed man in tight jeans and a black t-shirt walks toward me, looks me in the eye, and smiles before turning sharply and joining another young man in a booth. His t-shirt reads, "You are Not Alone."

Indeed.

This is what *Deep Midwest* is about. Recognizing meaning all around us, and sharing it in a way others might find interesting, even valuable.

The written word has always held my fascination, and I even remember the first word I recognized the meaning of—"look," in a Dick and Jane reader in Kindergarten. I remember my five-year-old astonishment when I realized that the letters and words on the page could represent an abstraction, and then together, tell a story. I quickly gobbled up new words as I encountered them, as writers wove them first into sentences, then paragraphs, and finally stories. Stories that transmitted me to indescribably delicious corners of the universe. Unimaginable places that seemed so much better than where I was in rural Iowa.

And stories were all around me. Everyone told stories back then; it was part of being alive. Not everyone had a TV, and there were only three television channels. Personal computers and smartphones were the material of fantasy. I reveled in the stories of my parents, aunts and uncles, and especially the stories of grandparents; stories of happenings so long ago it was nearly unimaginable. Stories of the great depression, wars, and events beyond my imagination.

There was little joy in school. Chained to our desks we toiled. I remember once looking out the window when a meadowlark broke into song, and I wept, I was so distraught I couldn't go outside.

My first F was in first grade. Not only was it an F, it was a dreaded "red F." Not only was it a dreaded "red F," it was such a bad red F that my teacher was so angry, the force of the effort of her pen tore the worksheet. I remember looking at the paper, its tender fabric pierced, scarred by the worst grade imaginable.

I clutched the paper to my chest, a total mess. It was a late Friday afternoon, and I hauled my shameful little ass onto the schoolbus.

I knew I would have to tell my parents, and my heart ached. I fretted about it all weekend. Honesty was a core value, and sins of omission—not telling my parents, were as bad, or worse than the original sin of commission—the red F. I put it off as long as I could, until Sunday night as we gathered around the television, and tuned in to Walt Disney's Wonderful World of Color. For some reason, hearing the Disney theme, "When You Wish Upon a Star," opened the floodgates, and I told my parents. I don't remember their reaction, but that probably means it was comforting.

I forget what grade I was in, maybe second, but my next low moment came when I got a D in handwriting. "D" stands for "dummy," you know, was what we said at the time. It was during the first grading period of the fall, and a nearly school year long year of punishment awaited me. To improve my handwriting I was required to practice during recesses and after school until I got a C. No recess! Extra prison time at my desk, while my friends were out playing. This was when we had a half hour lunch recess, and 15 minute morning and afternoon recesses. I alone, had to stay in for recess. No other transgression any other child had made was so egregious as mine. Bad handwriting.

To further my humiliation and punishment, I had to practice my handwriting for an hour immediately after school. The very best part of the day—ruined. While I was stuck inside, the other kids were out at the crick exploring, playing tag, catch, or some other wonderful game.

So, over recesses and after school for nearly a full school year, I practiced my handwriting. I would dutifully copy passages from the World Book Encyclopedia, or from the dictionary. Hour after hour, day after day.

Did my handwriting ever get any better? No.

But something else much more important happened. Copying randomly from the dictionary introduced me to wonderful words and concepts, expanding my vocabulary. The World Book Encyclopedia, the Internet of its time, took me to incredible places, introduced me to fascinating people, other times, and the flora and fauna of the world. Physics, geometry, Latin.

While my handwriting never got any better, my knowledge and appreciation of life, our world, and words and stories grew and grew.

There were wonderful times during school, of course, but each was like a tiny oasis in a great desert of boredom. During early elementary school, when the teacher would read to us, I was in heaven. It was always my favorite time of day. Later, we would have a reading period, which was always a great escape from the drudgery of school.

And then there was the excitement when the bookmobile came. Our school library was small, and our librarian sat at her desk like a troll guarding a bridge, daring us to try to check out a book. A student had once used a slice of bacon as a bookmark, and the poor woman was never the same.

But the bookmobile man was a joy. To me he stood at least seven feet tall, with a full head of white hair. Probably in his 50's. He was the only man I had ever seen wear a suit outside of church. He would stand at the door of the bluebird-blue bookmobile bus, arms crossed, with a pleasant smile as we kids approached. There was a door at the back of the bus, and we would enter one by one, browse the books, take what we wanted, and then move to the front of the bus where we would check out the books from him, and exit from a door at the front. We could check out as many as seven books at a time, and I would always check out the maximum. They were due two weeks later, and I would always have finished them all. Once, I was thrilled when he called me his "best customer." I remember when he started pulling books off the shelves of the main library in Des Moines to add to the bookmobile shelves so he could recommend them to me. "I thought you might like these," he said. I beamed.

I've always loved newspapers, and radio, as well as books. The Des Moines Register would arrive every morning, and the Des Moines Tribune in the afternoon. Mom and Dad would read the paper every day, and I would follow their lead. That's what one did. No one was allowed to touch the paper before Dad did, and he would grumble over breakfast and scold the paper and interpret the news for anyone within earshot. When he was done, I would read the paper for myself, and was always pleased when I found the articles so different than Dad's interpretations. There were great columnists back then—John Karras and Donald Kaul among them, and they shaped my writing style to this day.

They taught me not to take formal institutions, or myself, too seriously. They also taught me that writing with humor was the way to a person's heart and mind. And a good chuckle.

My third grade teacher, Mrs. Schneckloth, had us discuss current events every day. If I remember correctly, it was always the first 15 minutes after the school day began. It became clear to me that some of us knew way more about current events than others, and I felt comfortable contributing during discussion, when I rarely did on other subjects. One day, Mrs. Schneckloth said something like, "if I had to count on someone to accurately tell me about the news of the day, there are three people I can count on. I would first speak with X, then Y." Both were smart kids, and I wasn't surprised. What did surprise me, however, was when she pointed at me, and said my name. I was her third person.

With that bit of affirmation, I increased my determination to excel at my knowledge of current events. While I had an initial interest, there was nothing like a bit of praise to inspire. It still works that way, I think. For most of us.

Another big event at about that time also influenced me as a writer. The teacher—maybe it was Mrs. Ward in 4th grade, told us to cut a historic photo out of a magazine, paste the photo on a piece of construction paper, and then write about the photo on the back of the construction paper. I chose a photo of a painting of a Civil War battlefield that I cut from either Life or Look magazine. It was an idealized and romanticized image, with Union soldiers on the right, and Confederate soldiers on the left. Some soldiers were firing weapons, while others struggled in hand to hand combat; one brandishing a bayonet. Others were firing a cannon, and the dead and the dying lay on the ground. Floating above the fray was the wondrous image of Lady Liberty holding her torch, her swollen breasts nearly revealed by what seemed to me to be her nighty.

I dutifully pasted the photo of the battlefield portrait on the construction paper, and pulled down the World Book and started researching, and when I held some kind of order in my head, actually started writing. I researched and researched, and wrote and wrote. I moved from the World Book, to more advanced encyclopedias, and then into books that had been written on the subject. We were only supposed to write to fill the back of the one sheet of construction paper, but I had filled up several pages when it came time to turn in the assignment. I remember asking the teacher if it was OK if I kept writing on the topic. She gave me a puzzled look, but nodded. So, I kept researching, and writing, and did so through the end of the year into the next. By the time I finished, my research and writing filled several inches of construction paper. After that exercise, the basics of research and writing about it came second nature. Of course, I was a plagiarizing fool, but fortunately learned the perils of that in High School. Not that I paid any attention to the transgression until college.

When my uncle Jim came back from being stationed in the Aleutian Islands off the coast of Alaska in the early 1960's, he brought back a shortwave radio for me. It was a miracle. I could hear radio stations from all over the world. Much of the programming was in English, and I loved hearing about happenings from other countries. My favorite program was where a Japanese naturalist climbed Mt. Fuji, and taught us about the culture and natural history of Japan. Every day we would travel a few paces closer to the mountaintop, and the sound of his footsteps, the birds calling in the background, and the lessons he took from everything around him helped me eventually decide to become an anthropologist, as well as to pay close attention to the world around me.

We grew up just north of Des Moines, in an unincorporated area known locally as Dogpatch, after the town the popular L'l Abner comic strip. In the strip, characters were poor "hillbillies." Like those in the fictional town of Dogpatch, the couple of hundred people who lived there didn't have much. Electricity came to the area right before I was born, and most of us didn't have running water. We thought our aunt, who lived next door, and who had a hand water pump in her kitchen, was rich. Everyone had an outhouse, and it was no big deal.

Below us, Beaver Creek drained into the Des Moines River. There, in the floodplain was a kind of shanty town, where at least one aunt and uncle lived. There may have been "permanent" houses there, but I don't remember them. I remember structures made of pallets, plywood, and tar paper. Beaver Creek flooded regularly, and I remember at several spring seasons of us trying to help families get their belongings out before the flood waters claimed them. One memory has me standing in floodwaters halfway up my thighs, trying to help with smaller items, while strong men moved furniture into the back of pickups and open trunks. It was dark, and people were moving around me with flashlights, calmly. I could hear the sound of the waters moving around me, and the night sounds birds and frogs make in the late spring. I remember looking at my aunt as she helped carry things to safety, when a flashlight caught her face. I saw no panic, anger, or fear.

Just the face of a strong, resolute woman trying to save what was left of her material existence. I was maybe six years old.

About a mile and a half away and maybe 50-60 feet above us in elevation was the Meredith mansion. The mansion was built in the 1930's, by Edwin Thomas Meredith, founder of the publishing behemoth, the Meredith Corporation. The mansion stood on close to 400 acres, with magnificent twin barns, among the largest I've ever seen, to this day.

We lived in the shadow of the mansion, with little. Below us, people lived in a shanty town on the flood plain, with next to nothing.

That we lived in a world where some people had what seemed to be everything they wanted, while others have nothing, has bothered me as long as I can remember. At least since I was six years old. Probably five.

It still does.

All of these influences helped make me a reader, a writer, and an anthropologist.

Some of you likely correctly recognized from the beginnings of this piece, that I have Attention Deficit Disorder. You are correct. I was diagnosed as a young adult. Of course, when I was a kid, it hadn't been recognized. While I got average grades overall, I regularly scored well on the Iowa Test of Basic Skills, the standard achievement test of its time.

How did teachers explain the discrepancy? That I was lazy.

And that's an even bigger burden to bear than a red F.

Of course, college and graduate school were different matters; much more to my liking. Regardless, there are still kids in elementary school who weep when they hear a meadowlark, and my heart goes out to them.

Let's remember that we are all different, and sometimes our burdens may eventually turn out to be gifts. I think my ADD has let me see the world differently from the way many others do, and for that I'm grateful. But I'd still rather be outside!

WATERMELON

The watermelon appeared on the front porch one hot Saturday afternoon in September, sitting in my patio chair with dirt and bird poop on it. The melon was about the size of a basketball and nearly as round and it was green, not striped, and I looked across the street at the house and machine shed where Jim worked on his tractor and knew where it came from. I yelled for my little kids and we hosed it off, pulled a little yard table and more chairs off the deck and into the grass under the shade of the big elm out front.

I grabbed a butcher knife and created big chunks and we ate it with the juice running down our chins onto our shirts and I taught the kids how to spit watermelon seeds at each other and me and how to pinch them between your fingers and shoot them at each other and other things we had a mind to—including the dogs. We hoped Mom would walk out the door but she didn't. Asa, who is seven, said, "We sure are going to have a lot of watermelon volunteers in the spring aren't we?" And I said, "yes."

When we got to the center of the watermelon I pointed the big knife down and cut out a pyramid of the beautiful red seedless center and handed it to Johanna and said this is called the heart of the watermelon and it's for you. She paused for a moment giving that statement her four-year-old consideration it deserved, smiled and ate it. We ate that melon like wolves, threw the rinds and what was left in what Mom calls the compost heap and really isn't, hosed ourselves off, goofed in the yard until we were dry, and went back into the house to watch TV and read and Mom didn't know any different; she's never been fond of watermelon messes.

A few days later my phone rang and I didn't answer it, but listened to the message a couple of days after that and it was Jim and he said did you and the kids like that watermelon because if you did I have another one for you. When I saw Jim under the big trees in his yard on Saturday, I wandered across the road to his house, a hundred yards or so away, on the big round curve heading into town. His back was to me, as he was bent over the tailgate of his rusty pickup so I shuffled a bit in the gravel as I crossed the road so as not to startle him. He turned and said, "walnuts...shukin' walnuts."

With nearly black hands that one gets from walnuts, he worked quickly, peeling the crusty brown-green off. "Wait til the husk dries a bit and shuck it off, and let em dry, bake em in the oven and they're good eatin' especially in baked stuff. Cookies and things. Cakes." He pointed. "See all those walnuts on the ground there? Come on over anytime and take em home, I'm done with em and have this pickup bed full." He looked behind me and I turned to see what he was looking at. "Those two trees over there are pecans," he said and I looked and saw the pecan shells starting to dry and spread, opening like wooden blooms, nearly ready to drop their nuts. "Don't see many pecan trees around here," I said. "No," he replied, "they open and drop their seeds like hickorys do."

"Kids like that watermelon?" I nodded. "I have some more," he said, wiping his black hands on his jeans, and started into his backyard. "Never planted these watermelons," he said. "They just come up year after year. Must be volunteers from someone's garden years ago." Maybe a dozen watermelons were scattered across what looked to be an old garden plot. Tomato plants and gourds grew amidst the watermelons. "Volunteers. All volunteers," he said. He reached over and pulled at a striped melon. "This one's stem's dry. I guess it's ready." I took the watermelon from his hands, and it was warm from the sun, with dirt and bird poop on it.

"Don't get your shirt dirty," he said. I said, "it doesn't matter." We walked back to the pickup so he could get back to shelling walnuts. I set the watermelon on the edge of the bed of the truck for a moment, and glanced into the back of the truck. Six dead blue jays were lined up, like in a specimen case in a natural history museum. "Was feedin' those one by one to the cat, but just got too many," he said, shucking walnuts. "They was getting the pecans. Jays can clear a pecan tree in no time if you don't shoot em." "Shoot them?" I said. "Yep, challengin'," he said with a little smile. "Twenty two."

He continued shelling walnuts, and I wandered back across the road with the watermelon, wondering what the fine was for shooting blue jays, and thinking back to my granpa who thought blue jays were smarter and certainly more interesting than most people. I got home, set the watermelon in the grass in the shade of the elm, and went to get the hose. "Kids, come out here," I yelled into the house. "Watermelon!"

SECRETARIAL MIGRATIONS

Every weekday afternoon,
between five and six
thousands of little cars
mostly Tauruses and Cobalts,
pour east from Des Moines on Highway 5,
like geese, towards Pleasantville, Knoxville,
Oskaloosa.

And sitting alone in the cars behind the wheel
are multitudes of clench-jawed young women,
mostly muddy blondes, wearing fierce tribal masks of
lipstick, eyeliner and rouge, as they leave
their secretarial jobs in the big city, for lives
in towns where they can afford to live.

White knuckled, and shoulders tensed, their
heels and purses on the seats beside them,
some of them contemplate just what kind of misery
they are about to inflict upon the lovers
they might soon see, as they
corral the kids, cook dinner, and clean before
they can spend the rest of the night plopped on
the couch watching fuzzy network TV from the

big city, wishing they could afford the Dish Network
before they fall asleep, head on their lovers laps,
if they're lucky enough to have one.

And in the morning, they return like clockwork,
applying their masks in the rear-view mirror,
skirts up, driving with their knees.

BOY ON RED TRACTOR

95 degrees and I was on my knees
in the front yard planting a bush
that was maybe dead but I hoped not,
the hedge border Annie wanted.
Adding to the others.

She'd bought the three plants on sale
at Hy-Vee the other day, waiting for the next sale
and we might be able to complete the hedge,
before I was too old to dig anymore,
a real bad spot to be in.

And there he came, toolin' along
30 mph on a red and cream
Massey Ferguson,
from maybe the 40's or so,
not that I have a tractor field guide in my head.

He sat, long wavy blond hair blowing in the wind,
slouched and shirtless in Levis on the tractor seat,
maybe seventeen,
Bronzed and muscled.

On his way back from the field
I could tell, ready for the cool
of a Saturday night,
pushing what edges he could,
blue sky and cornfield behind him.

Then, as he passed,
he pulled a cigarette to his lips,
took a drag, smiled,
and nodded at Annie standing behind me,
maybe thinking of the girl
someday he'd be planting a hedge for.

AN EXISTENTIAL QUESTION

Five hours mowing grass with the air as thick as pudding had me about half done but outta gas and I saw the light on in the bathroom—just about bath time for the little ones—so I snuck up and rattled the window with my big old sweaty fist and watched them jump with glee at the sight of their old dad through the window, who they hadn't seen in a couple of hours, and before a buzzard could take off Annie was at the back door yelling, "What are ya doin you scarin' the bejeezes outta me like that," and she pointed at the ground beneath me and said, "and there you stand with your big feet trampling my wildflower garden beneath the window there." I looked down and sure enough I was standing on a bunch of violets and other leaves and twigs and stuff that I would have to take her word for it were there, but as I retreated I couldn't help but wondering to myself the existential question of whether or not a wildflower garden exists if a husband was never told about it.

122 TORNADOES

Saturday night 122 tornadoes more or less,
ripped through Oklahoma, Nebraska, Kansas,
and Iowa. Five died in Oklahoma, including a
couple of kids, bless their souls.

In our neighborhood an old couple's trailer rolled,
tossing them like two socks in a clothes dryer, and
five of our windows were blasted in, glassy shrapnel we
picked out of walls for months.

I walked ankle deep in hail at home, Annie's
irises shredded like cole slaw, dead birds
littered the lawn where they dropped,
punched from the sky.

Some of the tornadoes bore down for a while,
steady and focused, destroying towns, like a
rubber stamping Wells Fargo Mortgage
banker during W's reign, only from his cubicle.

Other tornadoes skipped, like schoolgirls across
a playground, touching down, tickling cows,
destroying barns, giggling. Sending people to
ground and basements like tornado alley
doughboys diving into trenches.

MALLET

Old man Grayson in his overalls, Red Wings,
and St. Louis Cardinal baseball cap grabbed my arm
at the primitive tool auction in Albia on Saturday
and said, "see that big ol' mallet over there?"
and I nodded, looking where he pointed at a
rough old wooden mallet that was not from
this world—but I didn't know that yet—that had
a hand-carved handle long as a broomstick
thicker than the skinny end of a baseball bat with a
blocky oak head nearly the size of a concrete block.

I took it in my hands, shrugged, felt its weight, and
turned its business end to the ready and imagined
driving something with it, a big tent peg maybe, when
Grayson said, "My granpa said before he died in '57
that that there mallet and those like em was used to
drive timbers plumb and flush in the old coal mines,
like the Golden Goose he worked in the old days near
Hiteman, and all these old boys here at the auction just
think that these are mine tools but these here wood tools
are slave tools we brought with us from the plantations,
or the idea of em anyway, 'cause the plantation bosses
didn't want black men with steel 'cause steel was too

expensive to buy they said, but really with enough time,
and they sure had enough time, a clever fella would make
a nice club or shiv outa steel and they didn't want that, no sir."

And he looked at me and I said, "Oh."

OLD MAN IN NEW SHOES

I watched an old man in overalls walk out of Casey's north in Knoxville in a spankin' brand new pair of white shoes that looked like some major brand knock-off that maybe he bought at Walmart at the edge of town. And as he shuffled across the stained sidewalk, mostly gum and pop and cigarette butts, he appeared comfortable in his new shoes, and I wondered if those just might be the very last pair of new shoes he would ever wear. And then I looked down, and wondered how many pairs of shoes I might be behind.

TARGET

Mom, who the doctors at Methodist had taken a breast off of five years ago, because of cancer, and who had been recently diagnosed with a bunch of new (to us anyway) cancers in different parts of her body such as pelvis and liver and spine and brain, so many that I couldn't keep track of, when the doctor told us gently with his hand on her knee, with my sisters riveted to his words in the hospital room, and my brothers-in-law nervously looking the other direction; today weak after radiation, she called me on the phone from either 35 miles away or a million I forget, telling me that she figured out how when she got out of the hospital she could help Dad keep up with his exercise—needed to keep his arrhythmic heart beating.

Dad, the guy who broke the state 100-yard-dash record in 1952, whose thick carpenter's knuckles, fat calluses and strong, brown right arm had driven more nails, mostly sixteen pennies and sevens, than stars in the Milky Way, whose heart had only half a beat from a heart attack years ago, that he had evidently gutted out not calling the doctor like a real man does in a culturally sanctioned dumb-ass way, from generations ago when the earth was young.

Mom told me that she figured that when she got home, she could help him get his doctor-ordered laps in, in a brutal January, walking beside him, offering encouragement as she leaned on and pushed a shopping cart she'd borrow for just a little while from the Target store, pacing her old carpenter bent not so much from age but from wear through his laps, at the Merle Hay Mall in Des Moines.

HOMETOWN MEATS

"There's some that likes the bone in and some that likes the bone out in them pork chops," said Mary the counter lady at Hometown Meats to the man at the counter.

"Sorry can't sell ya that there bag a charcoal sir cause it ain't got no price tag on it," said Julie the new checkout girl. "I can sell ya this Match Light though, cause its got a tag."

"Hamburger? Ya got yur ground chuck which is the best for patties and grillin' and this lean 80% for crumblin' in stuff," said Mary.

"Tastes like crap though," said Gil from one of the tables.

"You shut up Gil, it's better for your diet, though it tastes like shit," said Mary, "not that I said you should be on a diet though."

Shuffling through his change, old Marty in his overhauls and John Deere cap pulled out 42 cents and said "I'd like 42 cents worth of baloney please."

Mary cut it, and Marty walked out eating it, with a grin on his face like he was a kid eating a candy bar.

UNLOCKED

Three year old Johanna,
almost four,
holds onto the bathroom door,
that doesn't lock, and says
don't worry daddy, I'm just
holding onto the doorknob
till your done.

MILLER LITE

Duane the 70ish kewpie doll bartender at the Iowa Bar in Melcher was shakin' when I walked up to the bar and ordered a Miller Lite.

"Goddam," he said, "I wish you'd a been here an hour ago when the Bud man was chewin' my ass for adding a Miller Lite tap to the bar. Bud man said that Miller Lite was a pussy California beer, and no decent Iowan would drink it, and he said if I had to have it on tap, I could at least put it in the back room, under a towel, where no one could see it. Goddamn beer men are bout as bad as the chip men, each of em, rearranging my chips once a week putting their product out front, and cussing me for letting the other guy do the same. And so I said to the Bud man, dammit, it's my bar, and I'll pour whatever beer I want, and if you don't like it, just haul all your kegs, those damn Budweiser clocks and waterfalls and Clydesdales outahere, and well he had a change of attitude right quick for sure."

"Thank you," I said, taking a sip of Miller Lite.

BONE THIN

Our society
sure loves a bone thin woman
worships a bone thin woman,
exalts a bone thin woman,

nothin' more than gristle,
breasts and hair,
which seems a shame,
since voluptuousness
is so much more pleasant,
and easy to obtain,
in rich America,
even on food stamps.

But get just a bit too thin,
here in southern Iowa,
and we'll want to look
in your mouth, at your teeth,
sort of like buying a horse,
but we're too polite to ask,
and we'll just glance at you,
time and again,
surreptitiously,

looking for bruises too,
and those trembling shakes.

We ponder your corn husk crisp bodies,
about to blow away like dry leaves
on a windy fall day, twitching.
And we'll wonder if you're doing
the methamphetamine jitterbug,
windhumping.

OWL TAP 2007

Billy at the Owl Tap in Albia was only on his fifth beer when he leaned over to me and said,

"In my great-granpa's time way back in the old days after the Civil War, he'd a plowed his 40 acres with a mule, and when he'd a stopped to take a breath he'd a looked to the skies, licked his finger and holdin' it to the wind, knowin' he had no idea as to what the damn weather would do, to his corn and alfalfa, milk cow and gramma's garden on this damn hilly gully ridden land, be it rainy or not, droughty or not, hail or not, blizzard or not, windy from hell or not, he'd just shake his head and turn to the plow and keep on workin, knowin' nothin' bout the weather.

And now we all watch Doppler radar, plow thousand acre spreads, gettin' market updates, and hour by hour rain predictions on our smartphones, as our GPS guided tractors plant corn and beans and gather data, and while I can spend entire days watching Weather Channel simulations of counties topplin' like dominoes in that damn Texas drought, that's spreading this way, I'll still look to the sky be it rainy or not, droughty or not, hail or not, blizzard or not, windy from hell or not.

And just like great-granpa I'll look at the sky and just shake my head and keep on workin, knowin' nothin' bout the weather."

IOWA BREADBASKET

My romantic image of the Marion County farmer took a hit, when I toured the Cargill plant in Eddyville, and learned that the majority of our corn is turned into hi-fructose corn syrup, coloring to make chicken skins yellow, filler for dog food, MSG, and the totality of the world's supply of the active ingredient in Febreeze ™.

HURRICANE

Jessie sits at the end of the bar for a day or two
at the first of the month, after the welfare check comes.

Her husband Randy, with two OWI's behind him
this past December—the holidays you know—

Was caught on camera passing bad checks at Walmart,
and when he learned they had a warrant out for him,
he hung himself dead with a phone cord.

Jessie's alone now with four kids under the age of ten,
with a dead daddy and one grandma who cares.

Sometimes.

Even when it's almost closing time, and there's a
deficit of girls at the bar, and a good song is on the jukebox
no one asks Jesse to dance,

Because talk among the guys is a single man better keep
his distance from a horny woman with four kids to feed,
and a dead husband from suicide, though on the surface it
didn't seem that she would drive a man to it, but you never know.

And the bar TV was turned to Fox News, and we were watching the New Orleans Hurricane Katrina victims, and Jesse said, look at that—those folks got hatchets in their attics to chop themselves out when the flood waters get high and they reckon they about had it.

Marlene, the barmaid, took a puff and wiped down the bar in front of Jesse and said, gonna take you more than a hatchet to get yourself outta the trouble you're in, hon.

Jesse nodded, looked around the room and, seeing no man taking time to look her way, said ain't that the truth.

BOWL

It's dawn, and looking
towards the sunrise,
from the upstairs window,
cold air leaking in,
I see that the first snow of
November fell last night,

and that the 1,000 pound
bales of hay in the neighbor's
hay field look
like Kellogg's Frosted
Mini-Wheats,

leviathan,
sugary pillows,
afloat in a lake
of milk,

And sitting at the
edge of the bowl,
I wonder where

I put my giant spoon.

WIRED

If I weren't married to such a good woman
bustin' her ass working so hard inside the house
and out in the garden and everywhere else
in our world I believe that when I was
doing my ten hours or so of mowing every week
I'd be tempted to take a piece of gauge 10 wire
with me, and every once in a while wire the safety
bar of the mower tight to keep the mower going.
and it would sound like I was still working when really
I was sitting in the shade behind the barn or
the corn crib or some other outbuilding reading a good book.

Honestly.

TONIGHT'S THE NIGHT

Watching the late April rains come
and fill English Creek is mesmerizing,
and worrisome at the same time,
like watching a beautiful woman cross
a crowded room, catching your eye.

Thickening within its banks first,
then gently overflowing, oozing onto
fields, tickling the tires of the tractor
of some absentee landowner
between here and town,
threatening the bridge where
the kids and I found

the snapping turtle.

I was tugged back home,
by the ring in my pocket,

and Annie told me there was a foot of water
in the basement and what should we do.

So I went home, wondering just what kind of mess we had.

As the fields slowly drained, and farmers
worried that they'd be planting
late this year, Mike the Rotor Rooter
man unplugged the red clay
graywater lateral
that led from the house to the ditch and said,
might of been some animal crawled in there
a long time ago, that or someone's grandma's hair here,
pulling a mat out of the big snake's bit and
tossing it into the ditch with a big slap.

and I hauled the memories out of the basement in their soggy
cardboard boxes while Annie sorted them out in the backyard,
and I noticed that one dead mouse was laying on top of a soggy
Rod Stewart album called "Night on the Town."

From my perspective the mouse was hanging out of
shaggy-haired Rod's martini glass,
nose against a song title:
"Tonight's the Night (gonna be alright)",

And I laughed, and felt better.

SMALL MIRACLES

I

My little girl played alone, at the playground in Bussey,
seven years old, occasionally topping a piece of equipment,
perched like a sailor scanning the horizon,
longing for a playmate or two, on a summer's day.

And me, hunkered in the shade of a nearby tree
pretended to read, my heart heavy with her loneliness,
as she slid down a slide, climbed a wall,
hit the top deck of the colorful playground
built by donations, and the hands of townspeople.

Before long, with the conveyance of an invisible
magnetic force, like the instinct
that guides Monarch butterflies to and from Mexico,
or maybe it's something in the air, or in our stars,
in sailed half a dozen other girls, about her age,
give or take.

On their way to somewhere else, they paused
when they saw a kindred soul in the park,
all alone, and came to remedy that.

And they played. Prayers not voiced,
but answered.

II

In the old coal town of 500 people,
some dirt poor, the others lucky
enough to have a job at the Eddyville Cargill Plant
processing corn, or Vermeer, welding balers,
or Pella Corp, building windows.

And in their play, the girls found themselves
under a cherry tree, and somewhere
across the universe a star exploded,
and Albert Pujols hit a bases loaded home run
to put the Cards in the lead for good,
and maybe someone somewhere figured out
the final chord of next year's platinum hit
that a generation would sing.

But nothing, no nothing,
was as miraculous
as the girls picking red ripe cherries,

little girls picking from the bottom,
middle sized girls climbing the
tree for middle branch fruit,

and tall girls reaching to
the sky for ripe ones, to pass down
cherries to the girls too small
to reach any branch at all.

CRAZY LADY

Sunday morning Thanksgiving weekend
Allie the new dog that wandered in last August
gave a bark from outside that we didn't recognize and we
watched, from the window, three men in fluorescent orange
hats and vests with shotguns tucked under their arms move down
the brush strewn crick bed towards the house.

"Dead bird, Dead bird, dead bird," they mumbled
quietly to their dogs.

Annie grabbed her coat and flew out of the house like
a bat out of hell in slippers across the yard, scattering
juncos, sparrows, and woodpeckers from the feeder
in her wake. From the window the kids and I could hear
her yell, "Get off my land, you bastards!" And they
said, "Yes ma'am," and called to their dogs and wandered
away and up the hill through the bare earth stubble of the
neighbor's west cornfield harvested over a month ago.

And after awhile she came back into the house to the fire petting the dog,
kicked off her muddy slippers and said, "It doesn't matter to me if a
rumor spreads that there's a crazy lady at the old Turner Place."

And we said, "Yes ma'am."

FOOTPRINTS

The day after winter's solstice
the earth grew optimistic,
and the temperature
rose to almost 50
degrees.

And I went walking
through the melting snow and
mud through the south pasture,
just for walking's sake.

And I saw that I was not the
first to have the idea.

Deer footprints,
like hands cupped in prayer,
star shaped raccoon, or
maybe a possum too.

On my knees I spotted
tiny feet, mouse sized,
with the line of a tail,
dragging.

Looking back,
I saw my size 14's
following,

late for the party.

CUTTING WOOD

After a month or so of cutting wood in the grove across the gravel road, where the cattle find shade in the summer, I learned that even in the dead of winter, on a pale gray day, that I could tell a dead tree from a live one. By its bark, a subtle difference in color, maybe—and the way the dead leaves hung, limply, if it had any leaves at all.

I only cut dead ones, my Husqvarna and I. I knew that I had been cutting dead trees for way too long, when I went to the Hy-Vee grocery store in Knoxville for cold beer, pork chops, and applesauce, and started looking at the people at the Hy Vee like they were trees.

There were lots of young saplings behind the cash registers and bagging groceries. Seedlings were being pushed around, in wheeled pots with binkies. Old men in the liquor aisle, limping, backs bent, clutching their six-packs with gnarled fingers like twigs.

Blue haired ladies, sagging over their carts, as if bent by the weight of great vines and strong winter winds. Bloated ankles like heavy roots.

And over there by the motor oil, light bulbs, and bungee cords, a young woman stands next to her tall grumbling boyfriend. She turns, leaning away from him and towards the life-giving light that can only be found out of his shadow, but maybe not far enough.

Lucky girl, from here her roots look shallow.

THE OUTDOOR CHANNEL

Johnny at the barbershop in Albia was
clippin' my hair the other day, when
he got frustrated.

You and your wife argue over TV? he asked.

Not really, I said.

Well you're lucky. Darn lucky. My wife got mad as hell
the other night, just blew up, arms flailin'
and everythin' and then she says damn your old ass,
I knew I should have never married you,
you've been watching that piece a crap
Outdoor Channel for over ten years now
and I'm tired of it. Tired of it, I say.

All they do is kill deer, kill deer, kill deer.
How many ways can you kill a deer? What
more does one man need to know about how to kill
a deer? I think you know all the possible ways someone
can kill a deer, old man, includin' a shotgun,
a handgun, a slingshot, your bare hands, and dammit
you could bazooka it if you had a mind to

and I'm givin' you notice that we aren't watching
that damned how to kill a deer channel anymore,
no sir.

And she grabbed the remote and changed
the channel.

What did you do?

Just sat there.

What channel did she change it to?

The SciFi channel. Really wasn't that different though.
They shot a lot a aliens. In my mind I just pretended
they were deer.

Oh, I said. And he felt better.

NOT YET

Annie asked how do I know if the ice on the pond is safe to skate on? You know, she added, Shorty said that's what husbands are for. He's big and if you lose him you can get another one.

So on Saturday, after a week of temperatures under freezing, I wandered straight out onto the pond behind the house and lay my body down in the center of the ice, and looked straight up into that big gray sky, snowflakes falling, amazed by the wondrous geometry of it all.

Shotguns boomed in the distance, and I figured that it must be day one of shotgun deer season. The shots sounded hollow, like big steel balloons popping, and echoed off the hills, from far away and near, seemingly from every farm around and then some.

It would be still for a few moments, then boom. Boom. And boom again.

When I grew cold and stiff and just this side of the ice claiming me, I clambered up, careful not to slip and fall. I walked back into the house, brushing snow off my shoulders as I went through the back door, careful to bar the wind best I could from getting in.

Annie looked up at me from cooking and said, so, is it safe to skate yet? And I looked at her and then the kids and kicked my boots off.

No, not yet.

JOY

I pulled a box of wine from the cupboard,
grabbed a coffee cup like I always do,
and started to pour wine into my cup
using the handy plastic tap on what the
box says is the most popular wine in the
world—given it costs thirteen dollars or so
at the Fareway store, I'm not surprised.

As the wine slapped up
against the side of the cup,
like a burgundy tide, I noticed
that it was one of the new Christmas
cups Annie had bought for the
kids' hot chocolate, since we'd had
visitors and all for Christmas.

The white cups had a Christmas
tree painted on the side, presents underneath
the tree, and on the inside of the cup,
right where the burgundy tide rushed,

was painted maybe the most beautiful
word in the world.

Joy.

And I thought, how appropriate.
To pour wine into a cup that says—

Joy.

And I felt Joy, especially when
my cheeks first blushed, and the
wine began to gently caress my brain.

But then I thought maybe not
everyone in the world
got the same word on their wine cup.

Maybe some people got—

Woe

And to their infinite regret, maybe others drew—

Anguish

Or maybe even—

Ruin

Which of course, all made me think,

that I would probably be better off sticking to
hot chocolate.

But ever the optimist, I kept the cup.

And the wine in it, being never one to look
a gift horse in the mouth.

ROBINS I

Amidst the daffodils,
robins mate, flutter
then mate again.

Pausing often,
listening for worms.

Inattentive lovers,
multitasking.

BEST GIRL IN THE WORLD

Long before dawn as the house shook in the wind's grip of this cold February morning I shuffled to the perking coffee pot till I heard seven year old Johanna stir and quietly say "Daddy, may I have a drink of water?" and I pulled a ceramic mug from the cupboard and poured cool water from the tap and brought it to her, watching as she miraculously stirred from her covers and rose to take the cup, her hands touching mine in the glow of her night light. Briefly. Warmly. Her delicate sips took off on butterfly wings, then slowed, then stopped, and she handed the half full cup to me as she settled back under the covers and her small, warm hands held mine as she sighed and retreated into sleep. I kissed her forehead, felt her breath and whispered into her dreams, "You're the best girl in the world, the prettiest girl in the world, and the smartest girl in the world and no daddy in the world has ever loved his little girl as much as I love you." And I took her cup and drank from it as I walked away, slowly savoring her essence left in the water till the cup was empty and I pulled my shoes and coat and hat on, and went out into the wind and cold and darkness towards work, not noticing the weather anymore, her warmth, mine. .

DEER BLIND

Brady straps the new deer blind
onto an old shagbark hickory.
Up fifteen feet or so, deep in
the woods. Woods that stretch
from here to Missouri and more.

Straps fit snug to any tree
Just like the picture
on the box says.

Platform light space age
composite material.
The folding ladder locks in place.
For stability in mud or turf.

Place to rest your arm, cup
holder for a beer if one had a mind to,
not that we ever had a mind to—
just thought about it. Coffee for now
pouring it out a Grandpa's 50
or more years old Stanley®
stainless steel thermos.

New deer gun bought at the
big shiny Bass Pro Shop in Altoona,
where outdoorsmen go to shop and be seen
just like high school girls at the mall.

The new gun a Remington® Whitetail Pro
Model 770 Rifle/Scope Combo, camo
to match his Carhartt® bibs and coat,
(all the way down to his union suit),
Red Wing boots, all the best gear a
regular man can buy.

All fit for farm, field and town.
Just not for the big city.

And it's fall, when the deer
leave the cornfields for woods
headin down to the crick bottom,
cause the combines chase them
out, and there's nowhere to hide,
if you're a deer in a field a stubble.

And also cause the acorns are down.
and there's nothin better than
an acorn if you're a deer (well, unless
you're a buck then you'll choose
a doe).

And Brady's already prepared.
Been prepared for weeks.
A block of salt,
and fresh ears a corn dropped
every other day,
put 50 feet or so from the new blind.

Cameras with timers,
shootin' high resolution color
photos by day, infrared at night
"swinging the hunting odds in
your favor" (says the pamphlet)
by telling you who is moving when.

And just when Brady has settled
in, still on his first cup a coffee,
before he's even had to climb
down and pee once,

Lee the philosopher who wanders our
woods walked by, looked up,
and around and eyed Brady's
operation and said,

"My God, Brady.
Why don't you just fuckin' nuke em?"

EASTER

Easter morning after we fiddled with what the Easter Bunny had left, we went outside. The long grass in our unmowed yard was steamed asparagus green, frosted lightly by close to freezing temps last night. We walked below a robin egg blue colored sky, not a cloud as far as I could see above or around, and we were heading to Asa and Johanna's fishing pond to watch fish jump for the heck of it when wild turkey gobbles in the oaks and hickories sucked us in over there instead. Better than church I said. Hope so anyway. Kids nodded.

SHEEP DOWN

Abie and I sat sipping coffee at the bookstore about nine one morning, looking out of the big picture window. A woman walked by with her dog, a big mutt of some sort. A few minutes later three teenage boys walked by.

"Dogs are good people," Abie said. "Nothing better than a good dog. They'll take good care of you, be a good friend. Good company. Get a couple together though, they can get into some mischief. Chasing rabbits, squirrels, knocking a trash can over. Get three or more together though, and you've got a pack, and next thing you know you got a sheep down."

I nodded as the three boys passed by the window again.

"Boys are like that too," Abie said. "Get one of 'em, he's probably a pretty good kid. Helpful. Good to talk to. Good company. Two are probably OK. Get three of them together though, next thing you know you got a sheep down."

I nodded.

"Or worse," said Abie.

DECEMBER 15, 2012

Early Saturday morning driving home from the Falvey lumber yard in Albia, where that good man Joe had given me the lowest bid on supplies for repairs from the April hail and windstorm that ripped up nearly 500 homes in the county including ours, me taking back some roof edging, ice-dam and water shield, tar paper and other stuff—tidying up the project that shoulda been done so long ago that Annie probably wishes she'd of hired it out rather than me doing it. Clouds hanging low and rain—no, more like mist—coming down looking like snow maybe but not yet, any moisture being welcome in this damn drought and it just feels good to hear and feel the pulse of wipers on the windshield for the first time in months.

Driving north past the South End Tap in Lovilia and me thinking too bad it's not late afternoon so I could stop in for a beer and some good conversation, my cell rings and it's eight year old Johanna on the phone from home in tears, asking, "Daddy, why didn't you take me to the lumber yard this morning?" and I said, "Sweetie, you were asleep when I left, and I wasn't going to wake you up to go to the lumber yard," and she said, "Daddy, you know that where you go I go, except for work, even if you have to wake me up. I don't care if it's the middle of the night you wake me up, OK?" And I said, "I'm sorry and I'll be home soon and we can talk about it," and she said, "That's OK, daddy, I love you!" and she hung up, with a sigh.

And I drove the rest of the way home for another ten minutes or so with tears in my eyes, my heart aching for all those poor souls in the news we heard about yesterday, today and maybe forever, dead and alive, at Sandy Hook.

MAINTAINERS

The snow hit us just about right, six inches at the most, but hard to measure since the 50 mph winds had the National Weather Service calling it a blizzard, which sounds right to me, bringing us some drifts a few feet deep here and there and other places leaving nothing but bare earth, but timed perfectly for a white Christmas. And a white Christmas is rarer than one might think, about one in seven years, they say. And as always, the county road crews started with plows on the hard surface roads at four AM, allowing time for the wind to slow and the snow to finally lay down with the dawn, building some drifts that looked like lapping waves, and others like big fat dragon tongues. The maintainers, or what some call road graders, came out at seven to work the rock roads. And as always, the guys got to see things other people don't get to, like red foxes, and turkeys tracking deer, grazing where the deer's hooves break through the snow.

The day started warm, then cooled, so when the snow came Mike, the foreman, told me the rock roads were soft underneath the snow, making working the blades troublesome. The guys on the maintainers wanting to clear the snow off the rock roads for safety's sake, but not wanting to wreck very much of the 680 miles of road in the county by blading too deep into the muck. Rock roads can be delicate, believe it or not, Mike said, and one has to leave a proper crown and a good surface, while trying not to knock any mailboxes down.

And the guys went at a new snow again on Christmas Eve, working hard up to dusk to make sure that everyone could get home safe, that drifts were cleared, and that there were two lanes on every rock road in the county. Over the radio I could hear the guys talking more than usual, excited for Christmas coming it sounded like, and pleased that because of their hard work everyone could get to where they needed. To get done by dusk, guys who were finished with their routes in the south moved north to help where we got the worst of it, but not as bad as Des Moines—to say nothing of Ames.

The digital thermometer at the shop said 18 degrees and dropping, and right before dusk Mike told everyone it was time to "head to the barn, the roads were as good as we're going to get 'em," and for "everyone to have a Merry Christmas." For some reason as the guys came in and parked and checked their equipment, when done most hung around, not heading home, the camaraderie of the special day and general friendships they had held them in place, waiting till the last guy got in safe.

As they milled about the shop, one voice called out on the radio. "Sorry boys, I've got the hammer down, but I'm way out and she doesn't have much more in her."

"Don't worry," someone replied, "We'll leave the light on for ya, Elmer."

Written in appreciation of my friends, Marion County Engineer Tyler Christian, retired Marion County Engineers Abie Davis, and Roger

Schletzbaum, as well as Tom Wadle, Steve McCombs, Mike McMurray, and every other guy in the Marion County Secondary Road Department who work so hard to keep our roads safe in every kind of weather. Oh, and Rick and Denny? Keep my seat warm, will you?

PLAYGROUND

A young couple with no kids walking around the
Bussey Park, with its new playground equipment
bought with FEMA money and donations.

They saw the kids on the tall slide, and paused
to watch for a moment. Or two.

And they joined them on the playground,
smiling, as they worked their way in and
out of the equipment, hand checking every
nut and bolt.

For their safety, or maybe of that of other
kids too, or maybe the one in her belly,
or the one they were now leaving to go make,
as they left the playground, hand in hand,
after a long kiss.

BUTTERED BAGEL

Buttered bagel in hand.

Warm buttered bagel in hand.

Warm buttered bagel in hand,
I walked through the snowstorm.

Before dawn, warm buttered
bagel in hand, I walked through the
snowstorm.

Before dawn, warm buttered
bagel in hand, I walked through the
snowstorm, thermos of hot coffee
tucked under my arm.

Before dawn, warm buttered
bagel in hand, I walked through the
snowstorm, thermos of hot coffee
tucked under my arm, to
work on a Sunday morning
in a snowstorm, to my job

at the radio station, warning
people to be safe in the snowstorm.

Wondering, who invented the bagel?
Who invented the toaster?
And, who, miraculously a millennia ago,
conceived of the concept of butter?
And then there's coffee.
And radio.

All beyond the realm of
my comprehension.

As is, of course,
the buttered bagel,
warm in my hand,
as I walk through the snowstorm.

RED ANT

Spring storm heading our way
and me laying shingles on our
shed roof, still fixing shit
broken from last year's storm
that shredded roofs,
spring flowers, and pocked
vinyl siding like swiss cheese
across seven counties.

Ankles aching from working
the six pitch all day, I bent
to drive a nail with my old
roof hatchet, like real men
do, not like a new age weenie with
a nail gun, and after checking
the gray clouds galloping towards
me once more,

Against the crisp new
white shingles beneath me,
to my surprise I spot

a small red ant

a very small red ant

a minuscule red ant

walking purposefully
beneath me.

Was he lost, I thought,
a wanderer on a vast
desert of white, with
an ache in his heart,
throat thick from thirst,
a hollow stomach,

his eyes longing for an ocean of green,
and his homeland?

I wonder if his
Queen would miss him,
and climb to the
rim of her anthill, wailing,
calling his name, bidding him
to come home. *Please, please
come home*, I imagine her cry.

Or did he know exactly where
he was going, having been
sent on a mission by his Queen,

perhaps a scouting mission,
maybe to see what the
colossal human being was
doing on the shed roof, in his
old overalls, worn boots
and ratty, sweaty, ten year old
St. Louis Cardinals baseball cap?

And then I heard thunder,
saw a bolt of lightning,
and the rain started to fall
as I drove the last nail,
soft splats against my shingles,
growing larger, bleeding.

I clambered down off
the roof, careful not to
step on my friend
the small red ant,

the very small red ant,

the minuscule red ant,

on a mission from his Queen,
or lost, I don't know.

As I went to report to my
Queen, that the roof on the shed

Was done.

At last.

MONA LISA

Thinkin' that maybe we'd spook
a Great Blue Heron when
the kids and I
walked through the oaks
to the pond and didn't, but a
big box turtle did take notice
and slid down off a log into
the water with just a little
splash followed by a soft plunk
like maybe it was only an acorn
or maybe even a walnut dropping
from a tree.

And I baited J's hook with a plastic
jig, not wanting her seven year old
perfect fingers pierced by a sharp
metal hook any more than I'd want to
see paint splattered on the Mona Lisa.

OLD BRIDGE

I grabbed a footlong sub for five bucks
from Mary at Casey's south who tells me "You
don't want the meal deal, 'cause you don't want
to drink the pop, it's bad for your health,
and it'll make your ankles swell when you're
an old man, which you almost are, no offense."

And I drove over to the old covered bridge
by the pond to eat my sub by myself, because I
enjoy the company.

I picked the high point in the center of the
deck of the old bridge to sit on, on the fat 2 by 12
planks, worn by years of car, truck, and tractor traffic,
and probably even wagon wheels, wishing time
would collapse in on itself, and I could watch
all the people who'd ever been on the
bridge pass, like rewinding an old movie fast,
watching the regulars getting younger by the
minute, and the strangers driving by maybe just once,
with puzzled looks on their faces—lost.

And maybe even dozens of lovers. Or hundreds, who

sought the bridge in the deep of night to find a lovely,
quiet, and isolated spot under the stars, to woo.

It was the first hot day of spring,
over 90 maybe and the green was ripe
on the trees, ready to burst, popping
buttons almost.

And I ate my sandwich in the shade of the
canopy of the bridge, no one but me and
maybe dozens of kinds of bees—bumble bees,
honey bees, sweat bees, wasps, mud daubers
and maybe a bunch of others—

looking down toward the pond,
to the left a little, I saw a game trail, leading
into the timber and down to the pond maybe,

and I wandered down into it, following the red streak
of a cardinal, like a bright beacon to somewhere else,
sort of like Alice following the white rabbit into another
world.

As I followed the game trail, wondering what scent
I was laying down, odd mix of middle age man sweat, Old Spice,
bagel, bacon, dog, kids, peanut butter and maybe the vestige
of the perfume of every woman I had ever loved or even looked at,
until the trail got smaller and smaller, like stepping down into the
eyepiece of an ever shrinking kaleidoscope and soon I leaned down,

cause I had to, and before I knew it I was on my knees,
then knees and elbows, until I finally crawled onto
the black Iowa earth shore of the pond, looking deep into its one
big blue eye.

Then a heron spooked as I lay
my cheek against the cool clay,
and I listened to the pulse of the earth.
Hearing it I was 10 years old again,
wandering up and down hills and through cricks
all over the county, not a care in the world, not even
about lunch, the sandwich I'd left on the bridge, way back
a lifetime ago when I was middle aged.

Then a bullfrog croaked and I grew up again,
and wandered back to town, hoping no one saw the grass
stains on my knees and elbows, wondering how in the hell

I got that streak of dirt on my cheek.

PROMISE

Crows called from the treetops
when I pissed on your grave.

The first time I was at the graveyard
alone after I learned what you did
to that child years ago.

The burden carried all these years,
telling me just a short time ago,
a stone lifted from their heart.

And since I was a little boy, I never
did like you, your smart-ass superior
tone, the glint in your eye, you milking
your World War II greatest generation
bullshit before it was even popular.

And if your World War II service
bronze medallion wasn't already
lying there in the grass broken,
I'd of broken it.

Instead I spit on it.

And someday in the dark of night,
I'm coming back with my spade
and a hammer, and digging you up.

And I'm going to hammer your bones
to fine powder, and cast them to the winds.

And I'm going to winch up your tombstone,
into the bed of a pickup,
and drop it off the bridge into the lake.

And leave a deep, empty hole in the ground.

And if there is another life after this one.

I'm coming for you.

A TRIP TO BOSTON

At the Great Scott Bar in Boston,
tipping back my third Stray Dog
of the late afternoon, talking with a
bunch of working class guys and gals
I didn't know but did
because we all'd pounded more nails,
poured more concrete, turned more wrenches,
and busted more knuckles than
we had a mind to.

Thinking we'd better drink up before
the college kids arrived tote'n their
alternative universe, coming in at dusk
to listen to indie bands that were
coming in this week like:

The Ballroom Thieves, Snowden,
Bunny's a Swine, Shepherdess Pile,
The Pill, Huge Face, Krill, Tired Old Bones,
Pure Bathing Culture, Earthquake
Party, A Great Big Piles of Leaves,
Bleeding Rainbow and the Fat Creeps,

which are all better names than the
bands we used to listen to back
when the earth was young except
for maybe The Grateful Dead.

And me sittin' under the Elvis altar
framed by lava lamps,
reading a framed copy of the New York Post
from Thursday August 8, 1974
with the headline "Nixon Quits,"
next to a photo of young Richard Nixon—
which incidentally would make a great
name for a band.

Next to 74-year-old Johnny telling
me with pride that he had worked as many
hours this week as he was years old,
while slamming Subway "with
them advertising they had a cheesesteak
sandwich when everyone knows that Subway
doesn't even have a griddle, and you can't have
a cheesesteak sandwich without a griddle—
it's un-American by God!"

And when a guy tried to buy a round for his
table on a credit card, Kevin the bartender
pointed to a sign on the wall that said in big bold letters

"CASH ONLY. GREAT SCOTT ENCOURAGES
YOU TO LIVE WITHIN YOUR MEANS."

And so the group shuffled off politely,
apparently holding only credit cards.

And me looking into my wallet, and seeing that I had
a ten-spot and was OK, I bought another Stray Dog.

I left the change on the bar for Kevin when
that beer was done and gone, after a long
conversation about how the Sox were doing.

Which was good.

BURYING ANNIE'S DOG

I grabbed the round tipped shovel and the wood-handled file out of the shed because digging with a dull tool seemed a bit disrespectful.

I sat on the picnic table under the gazebo protected from the hot sun and filed not until the shovel was ready, but until I was.

Then I wandered out into the sun and put shovel to earth and cut the sod neatly, upslope from the bed of peonies, just where she told me to put the hole.

Young dog smart enough but forgetful enough that she chased a car from her blind side, and I tried not to think of the thousand dollar bill from the vet I was burying too.

When done I tamped the earth just right, backed off, and looked down at Annie as she planted flowers on the grave and wondered just how much of her I was burying here too.

WINTER'S END

As winter finally loosened her grip,
and a pair of geese were scolding
me for walking past their pond,
I noticed that of all the trees,
the young willows were the most
optimistic, their long, leafy fingers
bright yellow, almost the color of butter.

And then a breeze kissed me,
ever so sweetly, and the willow
leaves gathered in enthusiastic
applause, like cheerleaders.

For me, or the geese, I don't know.

INSURANCE

We all felt sorry for Jenny Troy,
and her three kids,
when we learned her husband
John was dead.

Shot and killed in a hunting
accident.

The men were drunk,
which didn't help—a case
of Bud Light empties in
the bed of his truck.

John was only 32, and
busy drinking beer and hunting
and fishing with his buddies,
buying guns, fishing poles,
camo, and other guy-shit,

that decorated his life
and antics along with the
kids birthday pictures
he could post on Facebook.

Showing off.

His drunken grin was so
damn cute, it was hard not
to click the "like" button,
though the drunk photos
with his kids were a bit much.

But John was way too busy
to pay the 21 bucks
a month or so it would
have cost him
to have an actual
life insurance policy,
plus, 21 bucks is a
case of good beer,
or a box of ammo maybe.

Too damn busy for that shit,
John was going to live forever.

But dead is dead, and so Jenny's
friends put out coffee cans
to put donations in at Casey's at both
ends of town, with photos of the kids,
to ask for help to pay some bills,
cause rent keeps coming due whether your
husband is dead or not.

A church collection was made too,
from a church they never went to.

And Jenny took on extra hours at the plant,
like that did any good.

But damn, even though he'd been shot
in the head, dead in that cornfield
near an old coal mine,
six months later
either John or his ghost rose up
from heaven or hell or wherever
the Lord sent him.

And from the grave he posted on Facebook
that it just really pissed him off that his wife
was now fucking his best friend, even
though he hadn't been dead that long,
and "Didn't she have some decency?"

Jenny gave the ghost's comment
a thumbs up, and posted:

"A girl needs all the help she can get with her

life insurance."

And she got "likes" all night long
from her friends, and we never heard
another damn thing from John
or his ghost again.

BOOK DELIVERY

When Sylvia the librarian, who delivers books to the home-bound, went on vacation and asked me to deliver books for her on Friday, I said sure, why not. "Can't keep people from their books when they need them," I said. And so I piled the stacks of books for a bunch of people into Annie's car cause it's bigger than mine, and my first stop was just south of the railroad tracks.

I knocked and an old lady voice yelled come in and I did, and she said sit down there, pointing to a kitchen chair, and let me shut off some noise, and she shut off her TV and computer. She said, "I was outta books so had to put on the noise. It's all noise, ya know," and I nodded.

Sylvia's notes said to lay out the books in front of her, one by one on her TV tray, and talk about them if you wanted, because she would like that, and it turned out she had a big pile of books some of which I had read, and we had a nice conversation and she said, "You're a book man!"

"Yes ma'm," I said, not remembering her name, cause no one remembers the names of old ladies. Old men either. "Gotta have books," I said.

And we talked about each book, just a little. There was a pause, and I was getting ready in my mind to leave, but she probably couldn't tell when she said, "My God, I love books."

And then she said, "I'm 84 years old and I was the oldest of six children. Raised in the south. And when I was but a girl every morning I'd get dressed and stand for inspection by my mother, and my day was spent doing nothin but what she wanted, cookin, scrubbin floors, changin diapers, laundry, and everything, cause she wanted me all ready and broke in for when I got a husband.

And so I did all that and back in those days they never let us girls run wild much, and so it was books, books, books for me. But I had to hide it sometimes, people would tell me I was wastin my life, nose in a book. They couldn't understand the love of books, and how sad is that. But I especially had to hide it from my mom, cause there was always work to do and she wasn't a reading lady.

And when I got older, I got to wander a little, cause mama said I couldn't find a husband at home, but it was only in daylight, because it was the south. Things happen at night, when no one can see you, some wonderful things and some terrible things and back in those days they never let good girls go out at night.

And now right here, those things that used to only happen out at night both good and bad are right there in front of us all the time on the TV and the computer. Right there in front of us, can you believe it?

And sometimes I wonder what's worse, going into the night for real, or putting it right out there in front of everyone on TV.

And sometimes I think maybe we shouldn't go into the night at all in real life or on TV. Maybe just let the books take us there. Just might be safer.

LIGHTNIN' BUGS

After dusk Annie walked in from her garden and announced, "The fireflies are here."

My midwestern linguistic sensibilities bruised, I harrumphed and said, "Those are lightnin' bugs; fireflies are what poets call them."

Annie grumbled back, "Well, this house is full of poets—come outside."

And so the kids and I joined her, and encountered a wondrous light show under the stars, with a cicada and cricket chorus.

Asa said, "Daddy, lightnin' bugs! Mommy, fireflies!" as he ran around the yard with four year old glee, chasing lightnin' bugs and fireflies.

PULSE

About the time that damn bouncy
red-tongued flapping chocolate lab
from some trailer down Story Street
decided to abandon his energetic and
erratic orbit around me as I walked
down the white rock road, I figured
that road rock must have been quarried at
the Durham Mine near Harvey.

About the time that my fresh cut
walking stick was thinking about
giving me a blister, I had convinced
myself I was glad that ditch water splashing
dog went home cause the last thing I needed
is yet one more dog to feed and care for
despite the fact I missed him. Already.

And maybe it was the about the tenth or
twentieth or so glacier melt cut hill I'd
climbed up and down and crick I'd passed,
with only one being bridge-worthy, as I
walked on that late March day as the water
was still flowing from the fields and greens

of various sorts peeking up from the side of
the road and even in it. Shyly.

And most of the fields were draining snowmelt
down long black plastic tubes, with the one I
was passing now still being drained by old red
clay tiles fired in some kiln far away, made from
earth I'd never feel in my hands or beneath my
feet, shaped by men I'd never know.

And I was thinking about the time that the
Durham Mine foreman told me that the underground
mine was so big that maybe all 30,000 souls in the
county could fit inside with room left over
to rattle around in, and that once the big haul trucks
went in they would eventually die there, and
never leave, and when I asked him if there
were fossils in the rock he told me maybe
but they dug so fast in the dark of the great
gaping maw of the mine we would never know.

"We just rip through them fossils," he said.
"Gettin' the gypsum. If they're there, anyway."

And then I heard the sound of waves lapping
against a beach somewhere far away from here,
maybe Hawaii, or Florida, or California.

Or the Riviera.

And I saw the red tile was draining water from
the field into an 18 inch corrugated aluminum
culvert running under the road and somewhere
underneath last year's brown grass in the ditch,
waves were building into hard, big pulses.
Clap-splash, pause, clap-splash, pause, Again,
and again. Not the steady draining down tiles
I was accustomed to, almost leaking, calmly.
But different.

And so I clambered down to look, my new
walking stick making a bad knee strong.
Just enough.

Sure enough the water pulsed,
out of the culvert onto rocks below,
against a deer backbone.
And a femur left by a poacher, for sure.

And I realized the only explanation,
for the strength of the lapping was it
was the pulse of the field, or maybe
even the pulse of the earth, with the tiles
and culvert being the veins of the field,
of the earth. Water, blood.

And I listened, and creaked my
almost old bones down, kneeled,

put my wavering hand on the culvert,
to feel the earth's pulse. Its waves
lapping below. And for that moment
I felt the heart of the earth.

And I thought of beaches that I had
known, in other lifetimes, tides slapping
against sand, and in my head I visited them
for a while, laying like a boy, in the warmth
of the ditch bank in last year's dried grass,
my hand on the culvert, warm from the sun.

Then I quit thinking, and pulled myself
away and walked down the white rock
road toward home, passing neighbor
John's boy, must be nearly 30 already,
going on maybe 15, who was shooting
new spring arrivals, red-winged blackbirds,
out of his dad's newly budding walnut trees.

No grin. Just all business, he was.

WORKMAN'S COMP

Bobby's cousin Becky's new granddaughter died yesterday afternoon.

Her daughter Carly's no good husband, Cody, was on workman's comp and played video games all day long in the living room with that six week old baby shut in the bedroom in that big apartment house in Waterloo, and the temperature gauge malfunctioned, and when Carly got home from her job at the beauty shop she found the little girl dead and the temperature in the room at 117 degrees and she came out screaming at Cody playing Grand Theft Auto on the XBox and he didn't want to drop the joystick long enough to call 911 till she unplugged the machine and started slapping him.

It's all over the news but no one wants to talk about it cause someone might feel worse than they already do.

ROBINS II

Except for the hearty ones that
overwintered, the robins arrived
by the thousands at the end of
February, taking to the fields,
and positioning themselves
evenly, nearly optimally placed
as if choreographed, but
timing a bit late, for the halftime
of the Super Bowl.

So focused, as they listen intently
for worms where the grass is
bare and muddy, between the patches of
melting snow.

Listen, stomp, stomp, stomp,
only to listen again, stomp, stomp, stomp.

Backs straight, attentive,
like the best students at the
front of the class. Or like
red-breasted nuns, dutifully
inventorying God's handiwork.

So studious, that I would
not be surprised to learn
that they had planned their
route home by consulting
Google Maps.

BISCUITS

I wept, after the first chilly day in September,
I posted on Facebook a photo of my lovely
seven year old Johanna, standing on a stool in the
kitchen, wrists deep in biscuit dough,
wearing a pretty sweater and smile.

I wept after I'd seen that a friend had clicked the "Like" button
on Johanna making biscuits—her own boy only a week in the
grave, him having sat up on the side of the bed, only to pass.
Covers still warm, just right, like biscuits.

POSSUM

Down the grassy hill, with bearded old man winter storm clouds behind him, came a possum. Like a bowling ball rolling slowly down the gutter, he wobbled down the rut of a nearly hidden cow path. A bright white star splattered his gray back, as if God's hand had tossed a genetic snowball.

Nearing the bottom of the hill, and the brushy crick bank below, he paused for a moment, looking back over his shoulder, as if he had forgotten something, or perhaps in regret. Sighing, he turned, shoulders slumped, and continued his journey, paying me no mind as he passed, and I continued mine.

GIFTS
(NOVEMBER, 2011)

When I first looked into your malachite eyes
so many years ago I forget, they drew
me in and I fell like a pebble down a well
except for the splash, cause I just kept
falling and have never hit bottom.

And I knew that there was something
ancient and wise in you that I would never
understand, but it didn't matter, because
I just knew that I had to be close to it.
In its glow. Whatever it was. And is.

And in my wisps of memory, I remember
driving up a hill and watching a girl walk
up the sidewalk, and me thinking in my
loneliness that I wished that I had
a girlfriend with a nice butt like that.

And then the girl turned her head,
and miracle of miracles she smiled
at me and she was you.

And ever since that gift of a smile,

you've brought me immeasurable
bounty. Much better than Zeus' gifts to
Copia, Fortuna, and Pax. The cornucopia.

Years of interesting conversations most
couples won't have in a lifetime
about issues both mundane and sublime.
Always thoughtful, if not always in agreement.

Miles of roads travelled, hand in
hand with each other, and sometimes
with ancestors, both yours and mine.
Time stands still, and flies.

Acres of understanding of my strange
Iowa man/boy ways. Sometimes
above and beyond your own best judgment.
Thank you.

And my God, the gifts of children,
first yours, then ours, then ours again. Then
lovely grandbabies. You brought your teeming
river of life up and over the banks, immersing me.
Joyfully.

And now I'm the luckiest guy in the world
pulling kid's bikes out of the driveway,
cooking spaghetti for the millionth time,
unplugging clogged toilets, hearing

Asa's story of Archaeopteryx yet again,
among thousands of the other small
joys of our good life.

And believe it or not, every time
I look into your green eyes, they still draw
me in and I fall like a pebble down a well
except for the splash, cause I just keep
falling and know that I will never hit bottom.

AIR CONDITIONING

"Air conditioning is for rich people," grouched my Dad in 1962 as he left our little house after sunset to pee in the outhouse or maybe in the weeds I don't know, and then find some cooler air and maybe a bit of breeze outside where he went to sleep on the picnic table hoping the mosquitos wouldn't be too bad before he had to get up at five and go pound nails to feed us—a 100 degree day behind us and likely more to come.

The cicadas and crickets, mosquitoes and light'n bugs and the moon did their thing while Mom, my sisters and I lay draped wide across white sheets dried by the sun earlier that day, in our beds in our underwear, arms and legs akimbo, cause skin touching skin makes sweat.

On occasion the air moved and the leaves in the trees whispered and it was bliss, but not often enough on those hot humid July Iowa nights. But even a breeze moving as slow as a snail offered hope, just like a kiss from a new love; you hope more are coming, but then you never know.

And now all these years later I'm staring at the corn and the moisture coming off it in waves on this 100 degree day, and our 23 year old air conditioner at home quit with a scream of metal on metal, Annie told me.

And I'm sitting here hoping that Owen, our heating and cooling man, can fix it, cause we sure can't pay for a new one and Dad was as right now as he was in 1962 that air conditioning is for rich people.

ARCHAEOPTERYX

Old farm equipment
litters the pastures like
dinosaurs in a museum.

Some of it I know what it
did, just like a child knows
intuitively the niche of a
Tyrannosaurus rex.

Others I'm puzzled by
and some day when I get
around to it and remember

I'll ask an old farmer
to explain them to me
when I draw them on a napkin
at the bar, or on a kitchen table
somewhere.

Sometimes I wonder if
it's better to know the answers,
or better to simply wonder
about old farm equipment
and Archaeopteryx.

SUNDAY MORNING

Sunday morning
Asa, Johanna and I lay in
the grass near the
black asphalt highway.
Warm.

Watching the clouds
both high and low, crisscross
in the sky, the sun struggling to
break through.

The young corn in rows
maybe six inches high
tap the tips of their
leaves, like fingertips
or drum rolls, to the wind.

Plowed black earth below,
honey locusts in bloom behind,
a turkey vulture mobbed by
red-winged blackbirds above,

as we all wait for the
thunderstorm, late to the party,
but sure to come.

BAR FIGHT

Two boys in painter's pants, work boots, seed caps, and paint all over them got into a tussle and popped each other a couple of times at the Iowa Bar in Melcher before old Duane tossed them into the street.

"Wow, that was quite a fight," said Emily, in her new black Hawkeye t-shirt and butt tight Levis, having a Coke before her shift at the restaurant.

"Shit," said Candy from the bar, setting her beer down. "That was nothin'. The worst fight ever in here was July 73 during Coal Minin' days and these nice black folks from Des Moines come in for a beer and wasn't causin' no trouble when that asshole Rudy Meyer walked in, saw them, and he said real loud like, 'my God. Time flies. Coon season already!'

And the nastiest fight I ever saw came out a it, and God, it must have lasted five minutes or so, which is a hell of a long time for a bar fight, and there must have been a dozen guys getting it on and breakin' shit till Duane here stopped it."

"My God, that's terrible," said Emily. "Those poor people... but Duane stopped the fight?"

"Surely did," said Candy. "Went out to his truck and started up his chainsaw and waded into the crowd and they all ran like hell."

Both looked at Duane, who was wiping down the bar.

"Yep, worst fight I ever saw," said Candy, taking the last sip of her beer, then setting her glass down.

"Husqvarna," said Duane, reaching for Candy's glass to pour her another.

GIRL SHOVELING SNOW

The gray clouds rolled in and out in just a few hours over the course of the January morning, shoved out of town by a big, deep blue sky.

A blanket of snow covered the earth once more that winter, and it was just below freezing, which may as well be warm compared to the way below zero cold of last week, with the wind on hummingbird wings.

As I was leaving town, I saw a girl in gray, with a bright scarf around her neck shoveling a driveway, slowly, deep in thought, with a great big smile on her face.

I wondered what that big smile was all about, and though I wanted to, I knew better than to stop and ask, and she'd already made my day, anyway.

So I went on home, put on my boots and stuff, grabbed my snow shovel and put on a bright scarf around my neck, and shoveled the drive, slowly, with a big smile on my face.

I thought maybe people would drive by and consider why that big guy shoveling snow had a smile on his face.

And though I knew it was unlikely that I would make anyone's day as they drove by and saw me, it didn't hurt to try.

FORD'S SOUTH END TAP

Things were rocking at Ford's South End Tap
in Lovilia early Saturday night. The band was
setting up and the girls were starting to gather around
blonde Jimmy in his Orange Remington Country shirt
at the Big Buck Hunter II video game,
much to the chagrin of Little John who was kickin'
lots of pins on the Silver Strike Bowling game beside him,
only to be ignored.

Two old boys in Carhartt overalls and coats were starting
to sag, getting sloppy drunk, telling tales about the old days
sitting beside the stuffed bobcat and under the wood
"Hunter's Fisher's and other liars sit here" homemade sign.

Country was playing on the Jukebox and the cute
waitresses in tight levis and t-shirts were blowing in the
breeze like grass to the music smoking like chimneys,
forever young.

When a 40ish woman with blow dried hair and more split-
ends than not, seven rings on her hands like brass knuckles and
a glittery t-shirt that said,

"I WAS A SLUT WHEN THE WORD MEANT SOMETHING"

burst through the door and heaved her magnificent bosom on the bar and yelled, "I'll have the balls of any man, and the man of any woman who buys my man Charlie any Jagermeister shots tonight!"

But I think the only one that heard her was me, and I didn't even know what a Jagermeister shot was.

THE LONG SNAKE

Every morning between 4:00 and 5:15 or so when you probably aren't even up yet, a line of cars and trucks snakes northbound on T-17 to the good jobs at Pella Corp, Vermeer, PPI, Van Gorp, and American Wood Fibers and other great U.S. manufacturing firms in Pella. Some of these rural straphangers begin their daily trek two hours south in Unionville, Missouri, and other points in between—like Centerville, Albia, and Lovilia.

Little spots of nowhere, once little spots of somewhere, till Earl Butz, Big Ag, and the "Green Revolution," of Iowan Norman Borlaug, hero or well-meaning villain, take your pick, took the small family farm off the map, with the big bloody breech birth of big Ag. Norman and the rest of Iowa, either busting ass to keep the hungry people of the world from starving, or destroying the earth with pesticides, herbicides, anhydrous ammonia and pig shit to bring the world an ocean of corn syrup for our Cokes. Or maybe both.

But some are still struggling out here, and kids go hungry in the breadbasket of the world, and pundits are arguing if there a "food" problem, or an "income" problem. I'd like to trust the economists to figure out, if only the ideologues would get out of the way of science. But until science is the prom queen, the good jobs are worth driving for, and slowly the long snake fattens, picking up numbers on Highway 5 till we take that right turn on T-17 south of Attica, where the 2008 tornado ripped those folks a new one, rolling trailer homes like dice and throwing grain dryers and roofs into trees to hell and back, and one house into a pond, mom and kids still sleeping, lucky to be alive today, Dad out early in the belly of the snake.

Through corn and beans we go, up and down hills, weaving in and out of giant slag heaps from the open pit coal mines dug 50 years ago, and underground mines carved 100 years ago or more, and bootleg dog holes from who knows when, nature only beginning to reclaim its advantage.

Past the landfill, where in a couple of hours garbage trucks from four counties will flit in and out like sparrows at a mud puddle.

Stopping extra long at the stop sign where we cross Highway 92, looking both ways twice, then again, and maybe again, because the devil dulls our senses there, fuzzes our brain, dims our eyesight, T-17 and 92 being the county wormhole of death, at least ten dead or maimed here over the past decade.

Past the bright lights of the Durham Mine, where fossil rich gypsum and limestone is pulled from the earth to become roads we drive on, where giant mining equipment goes to live and die, gargantuan metal creatures abandoned in the tunnel they break down in, never to see the light of day. Modern fossils. Just not yet.

Slowing down just enough not to bottom out when we cross the Burlington, Northern and Santa Fe tracks, conductor-less trains hauling black tank cars, pulling ethanol from the Eddyville Cargill plant to the gas stations of America and your gas tank.

Watching out for the deer we know we're going to hit someday, as we go down into the Des Moines River Valley, past the old sandbar beached steamboat wreck that pokes up now and again when the river is low, entropy and erosion pulling it apart, a new generation discovering it again every ten years or so, the past forgotten, more to forget every year, an old farmer told me once.

Up and down the roller coaster hills of Elevator Road, every once in awhile seeing the stacks at Pella Corp rising like a church steeple, clawing up toward the manufacturing gods.

And as we crest the big hill coming into town, playing the Pella PD lottery, hoping the Osky inbound traffic slows down on our own Elevator Road/163 mixmaster, all of us in our own little white line trances, while Jimmy B, who staples window screen into door frames eight hours a shift, all night long, is dreaming of someday putting his bottle down, saving some money, buying a boat, and floating down the river to come what may, saying, "Ain't life grand."

A GREAT MANY IOWANS

I have known a great many Iowans in my day. They include a man who built great sailing ships over a century ago, a home-coming queen with a beautiful smile and polio, a sculptor who uses butter as her medium, a hooker who works the streets of Des Moines because she doesn't believe in welfare, a reformed drunk and truck driver who found God and became Governor and might have been President, a 20-year-old friend who I wish had talked to me before he hung himself in 1974, a 65-year-old woman from Pleasantville who seems 16 when I look into her eyes, a retired merchant marine who changes the world one letter to the editor at a time, an old man in an engineer's cap who makes ropes at county fairs so children can learn the old ways, a man who washes chicken heads down a drain in Waterloo, enough Olympic medalists and All-Americans in wrestling to fill a bus, a cattleman from Oskaloosa who believes that cows belong in green pastures and not feedlots, a mayor who lays awake at night trying to figure out how to bring an ethanol plant to his town, a single mom who home-schools nine kids in a trailer with the guidance of God, a gentle man who loved appaloosas and blew his brains out when his wife left him, a book-loving doctor with four unpublished novels in a drawer at home who will write forever, a woman who teaches children of all ages how to ride bicycles at the state hospital in Woodward, a woman who buys organic produce for HyVee who believes going organic is liberal nonsense, a boy in Ritalin chains, a man on TV with a dog puppet, a philosopher from Sioux City who believes that you and I exist only to serve as background to his own existence, a professor who teaches the world about Neanderthals from Iowa City, a man who chose to study criminology and social work in college after his little sister was murdered when he was 14, a sniper in Vietnam burdened with images that flip through his mind day and night like a slide show, a former wrestler at UNI who teaches cowboy poetry at a university in Arizona, a couple who danced the night away at the Surf Ballroom in Clear Lake the night Buddy Holly, Ritchie Valens, and the Big Bopper crashed and died, that same couple who cried together the next morning, changed forever, a farmer who knew the world had gone to hell when hay bales got too big for one man to lift, a 60ish woman who played half-court girls basketball on the guard side of the court who could still cover Kobe better than half the NBA, a car thief from Keokuk, a concrete salesmen whose face beams when he's told his adopted daughter looks just like him, a girl who pours beer in a small town bar who thinks we don't know that she has a meth problem, a heating and cooling man who collects Corvettes and ex-wives, a young man who chooses to build an elaborate and successful existence for himself on Facebook rather than in the real world, an old carpenter with big knuckles, a gruff demeanor, and a huge heart, a fallen lawyer who picked himself up and found success on the sales floor at the Home Depot in Ames, a young man fighting in Iraq, a gentle and forgiving Lutheran minister who wrote beautiful poetry for us all, and another who took lascivious pleasure in looking down from the pulpit and scolding generations of us for being sinners, a time traveler from the 60s still drinking Boone's Farm wine and smoking ditchweed, a television newswoman so focused on work she lives in a dumpy hotel in Urbandale, a successful restaurateur whose parents came from Mexico fifty years ago to pick sugar beets near Mason City, a successful restaurateur whose parents came from Italy a century ago to mine coal in West Des Moines, a man I suspect murdered his brother, the first black president of a national bar association, five cops who beat a man down with nightsticks in an alley, a man who cheats at cribbage, a trumpeter in the Navy band, and a former priest still saving souls and fighting for you and me and our way of life even as they toss him in jail for protesting, as well as thousands of other Iowans who take what life gives them and then make choices.

Those are some of the thousands of Iowans I have known. I hope that I will know many more. Maybe even you.

Look for love, and when you find it, hold its warm and tender hand in your own, gently.

TRUST THE IOWA LOCALS

I approach my political writing much the same as I do my other writing, only in my political writing, I know that I must see things from a different angle than any other of the likely dozens of reporters that will be there. I know I won't be the best, or the fastest writer; I just like to offer a different perspective. Most of my political writing is for the New York Times *and the* Kansas City Star. *Here is one of my favorites—Trust the Iowa Locals. It appeared on January 25, 2016 in the* New York Times.

Pella, Iowa — "There he is!" I said after spotting the crowd near the fountain, a couple of dozen media minions, holding cameras and microphones, all waving for attention. Jeb Bush was in my Iowa neighborhood, and I needed an interview. That's what I do. I'm a small town radio news guy.

I report on everything — community events, City Council meetings, car wrecks, the occasional drug bust, murder or tornado. When I was asked if I was worried about satellite radio taking away our listeners, I told them I'd worry as soon as I saw Howard Stern at a local City Council meeting.

Since 2007, I've been covering the Iowa caucuses. Those weeks when our local news becomes your national news. We do our best to put the candidates through their paces.

And here I was, about to let my listeners down. In a few hours Mr. Bush was to give a speech to several hundred locals, and his staff had told me over the phone that they "hope" I understand that he is "way too busy" for an interview.

Still, I elbowed my way through the crowd. Security looked me up and down, then ignored me. Must be my suspenders, I thought. I parted some branches, finding an opening in the crowd by the trunk of a tree, to see who was interviewing Mr. Bush.

It was Mr. Big himself — David Muir, the anchor for "World News Tonight" on ABC. I sighed. Of course Mr. Bush would deal with the big media first — for many candidates and their staff, that's all they know.

I saw a friend who works for a local newspaper. He grabbed my arm and whispered, "You get Bush yet?"

"Nope, he's too busy," I said, perhaps too loudly. A lady holding a boom mike scowled at me, finger to her lips.

We watched Mr. Muir lead his interview, as dashing in person as he is on TV. Maybe more. Perfect hair. Teeth. A genetic miracle. His blue suit fit perfectly. Glancing around, I caught our reflections in a shop window. Thank God for radio and print, I thought.

I'm not sure how many presidential candidates I've interviewed over the years. Too many to count. Some of the candidates resonated with Iowans, others didn't. In 2008, Barack Obama and Mike Huckabee got some love; Joe Biden, Hillary Clinton, John McCain and Rudy Giuliani didn't. Some play the media like a violin, others are clueless. Some understand how crucial local coverage is, others don't.

I remember back in 2012 when Sarah Palin was still considering running. She was in town making an appearance and her security waved me through. Later that evening during a pause in activities, I asked the security director why he let me approach. "The suspenders," he said. "And wrong side of 50."

In 2008, Joe Biden was great. He made all of us small media guys and gals feel as if we'd known him forever. Joe was never in a hurry. Never "too busy." Hillary? "Too busy." She occasionally dipped her toe into the waters of rural Iowa, but preferred our larger cities. (Yoo-hoo, Hillary! I'm right here!)

Mitt Romney gave me a couple of interviews, but his staff wouldn't let him out of arm's reach, and I felt as if I was a quarterback with a mike in the middle of a football huddle.

In 2012 Rick Santorum was around so much, it was like he was a neighbor. He fit in just fine — sweater vest and all. In 2007, Chris Dodd, a Democratic senator from Connecticut, moved into the state, but it didn't help him. He looked too much like lots of city folk do: afraid he was going to step in a pile of cow poop.

At a summit on agriculture in Des Moines in 2015, when all the original candidates were in the race, Republicans seemed to know very little about agriculture. Mr. Bush, George Pataki and Rick Perry were somewhat conversant with agricultural issues. The rest appeared to think food magically appeared on grocery-store shelves. The national media, from what I could tell, were equally clueless. Every corner of this country is different. People in Montana might be concerned about the loss of glaciers in Montana. In California, the drought. In Louisiana, the oil industry. In Texas, border issues. In coastal New England, the fishing industry.

Martin O'Malley had to Google the price of corn and beans — not a good thing to have to do in Iowa. Lindsey Graham knew the price of corn and beans, but not much else about Iowa's economy.

Years ago, I remember Mr. Obama made a lot of time for locals, and answered our questions. All of them. Why had Mr. Obama singled us out rather than someone with big names? "You are the media who live here," a staffer told me, "who the community knows and trusts."

In local media, most of us have worked hard to be respected in our communities. People know our personalities, our biases, and are interested in how the candidates interact with us. Sure, the big media asks great questions about the economy, foreign affairs, health care, you name it. But my questions might be a little different, like, what do you think about the low prices of corn and beans? What can be done about the deteriorating lock-and-dam system on the Mississippi River that stops us from getting the soybeans to China they so desperately want? I know what Iowans want asked because I'm one of them.

Back at the Jeb Bush scene, he was being ushered to another event. I left my perch near the tree and followed. It felt as if Mr. Bush and his entourage had the whole production choreographed, and I was the only one who didn't know the dance steps.

I cut back between two parked cars and popped up in the path of Mr. Bush on the sidewalk. "Who are you?" he asked.

"Bob, local radio," I said. He nodded, and I went on. "One failed corn or wheat crop and the American economy collapses. Is agriculture a national security issue?"

Around us the media paused. Everyone searched for the camera angles they wanted. I sucked in my tummy and tried to stand up straight.

"Why, yes, it is," he replied slowly. But he had no specifics. It was a question, apparently, he'd never been asked before. A staffer tapped his watch, pulling Mr. Bush away, and the rest of the media followed. I knew that I had gotten all I was going to get.

ACKNOWLEDGEMENTS

First, I need to thank Annie, who has been bringing me never ending gifts from the moment I met her that continue today. None of this would have been possible without her. Asa and Johanna and my love for them permeates everything I do. They have grown into confident and talented young people who I know will continue to make the world a better place. May they continue their generous, kind and creative lives wherever they go, and live their dreams.

Johanna gets credit for the book's title. We were driving somewhere together, and I was telling her about the book, and that it needed a title, and she gave it to me. Deep Midwest. I like it.

My family members currently living as far away as Washington, Colorado, New Mexico and Massachusetts, and as close as Iowa, have my love and appreciation. I just wish I could see you more often. Although I may not be there with you, every day I think of each and every one of you. And Dad, I think you will enjoy this. Thanks for everything.

Thanks also to Mel & Holly Suhr at M&H Broadcasting for a wonderful job that gives me the opportunity to meet so many people.

My deep thanks and appreciation to publisher Steve Semken with Ice Cube Press. Steve has published more books by Iowa authors than any other press, by far. He's given a great many Iowans a platform on which to stand, and share our vision and construct our narrative about who we, as Iowans are. And what Iowa is, as a place to be. Thank you, thank you, and thank you.

Thanks also to copy editor Kaylee Kirpes, wise beyond her years. Copy editing poetry and some non-conventional prose isn't easy, but she excelled. She also pointed out errors of logic, agreement, and perspective. She also went beyond what most copy editors do, which is to point out where something is missing, could be clearer, and how to make it better. Her marginal notes were valuable assets as I worked to bring the book to a rest.

Next, I have an old friend I'd like you to meet. He's Jerry Green. I've known him for a long time too... I use this joke whenever I introduce Jerry when he comes to town, and he always leans back and laughs like it's the first time he heard it. We've been friends since elementary school, and the friendship never wanes. It was forged on the playground, in Boy Scouts, the football field, and on construction sites when we were young, strong and invincible. Today, we meet about once a month for coffee or lunch, and catch up on family, friends, and world events. We tell the same stories to each other we've told a hundred times, with as much meaning as if it were the first. And sometimes we just sit there, comfortable with each other's company. Look up best friend in the dictionary. That's Jerry's picture.

And thanks to you too, dear reader. I hope you enjoyed *Deep Midwest*.

Note: "A Great Many Iowans" appeared in *Iowa: The Definitive Collection*, Z.M. Jack, ©2009, Ice Cube Press, North Liberty, Iowa.

Robert Leonard graduated from Johnston High School in 1972, and received his BA in history from the University of Northern Iowa in 1977 and his MA in Anthropology from the University of Washington, Seattle in 1983. He received his PhD in anthropology from the UW in 1986. He worked in historic preservation for the Zuni Tribe in New Mexico in the mid 1980's until accepting a position teaching in the Department of Anthropology at the University of New Mexico in 1987 where he taught until 2005 when he and his family decided to return home to Iowa. He has also conducted field research in Washington, Oregon, California, Arizona, New Mexico, and Mexico. He and his family have lived in Marion County since 2005. He is the author of dozens of scientific books, papers, and newspaper articles, as well as an unusual ethnography (short stories and poetry) of the taxi cab industry in Albuquerque titled *Yellow Cab* (University of New Mexico Press 2006). A play based on the book opened on May 30, 2008 at the Adobe Theater in Albuquerque and played for 12 sold out performances. Another version of the play was performed at Central College and the Des Moines Social Club in 2012.

He is a frequent contributor to the *New York Times* and the *Kansas City Star*, and in the past has written for *Salon* and *The Hill*.

An additional interest is the anthropology of work, and over the years he has been a carpenter, taxi driver, roofer, bartender, car salesman as well as a professor.

Currently, he is News Editor for KNIA KRLS radio in Knoxville, Pella, and Indianola where he coordinates news as well as hosts special programming and the daily news and public affairs program *In Depth*. Over the years, he has interviewed nearly 8,000 Iowans.

The Ice Cube Press began publishing in 1991 to focus on how to live with the natural world and to better understand how people can best live together in the communities they share and inhabit. Using the literary arts to explore life and experiences in the heartland of the United States we have been recognized by a number of well-known writers including: Gary Snyder, Gene Logsdon, Wes Jackson, Patricia Hampl, Greg Brown, Jim Harrison, Annie Dillard, Ken Burns, Roz Chast, Jane Hamilton, Daniel Menaker, Kathleen Norris, Janisse Ray, Craig Lesley, Alison Deming, Harriet Lerner, Richard Lynn Stegner, Rhodes, Michael Pollan, David Abram, David Orr, and Barry Lopez. We've published a number of well-known authors including: Mary Swander, Jim Heynen, Mary Pipher, Bill Holm, Connie Mutel, John T. Price, Carol Bly, Marvin Bell, Debra Marquart, Ted Kooser, Stephanie Mills, Bill McKibben, Craig Lesley, Elizabeth McCracken, Derrick Jensen, Dean Bakopoulos, Rick Bass, Linda Hogan, Pam Houston, and Paul Gruchow. Check out Ice Cube Press books on our web site, join our email list, facebook group, or follow us on twitter. Visit booksellers, museum shops, or any place you can find good books and support true honest to goodness independent publishing projects so you can discover why we continue striving to "hear the other side."

Ice Cube Press, LLC (est. 1993)
North Liberty, Iowa, Midwest, USA
steve@icecubepress.com
twitter @icecubepress
www.icecubepress.com

to Fenna Marie
your thoughtful caring &
loving zest for life are
truly Deep Midwestern.